THIS CANDLEWICK BOOK BELONGS TO:

_____

_____

_____

_____

For Finbar
and Jock

Copyright © 1994 by Flora McDonnell

First U.S. paperback edition 1996

The Library of Congress has cataloged
the hardcover edition as follows:

McDonnell, Flora.
I love animals / Flora McDonnell.—1st U.S. ed.
Summary: A girl names all the animals she
likes on her farm, from Jock the dog to the
pig and her piglets.
ISBN 1-56402-387-7
[1. Domestic animals—Fiction.]   I. Title.
PZ7.M478434Iaac   1994
[E]—dc20   93-2463
ISBN 1-56402-672-8 (paperback)

10 9 8 7 6 5 4 3 2 1

Printed in Hong Kong

This book was typeset in New Baskerville.
The pictures were done in acrylic and gouache.

Candlewick Press
2067 Massachusetts Avenue
Cambridge, Massachusetts 02140

I Love Animals

Flora McDonnell

CANDLEWICK PRESS
CAMBRIDGE, MASSACHUSETTS

I love Jock, my dog.

I love

the ducks

waddling to
the water.

I love the hens
hopping up
and down.

I love the goat

racing across
the field.

I love the donkey

braying
"hee-haw!"

I love the cow
swishing her tail.

I love the pig with

all her little piglets.

I love the pony

rolling

over

and

over.

I love the sheep
bleating to
her lamb.

I love

the cat

washing her
kittens.

I love the turkey

strutting
around
the yard.

I love all
the animals.

I hope they love me.

FLORA MCDONNELL graduated from art school in 1989, and has since had numerous showings of her work, including an exhibit of artwork portraying the scenery and people of Glenarm, the valley in Northern Ireland where her family has lived for five hundred years. Also the author of *I Love Boats*, she was inspired to create *I Love Animals* by her own pets, which have included lambs, dogs, ponies, rabbits, cats, hamsters, and a family of crows.